THIS IS NOT A DINOSAUR!

For Andreas Österberg, who was timely and generous with his encouragement, and still keeps us company in our memories – B.T.

For all the dinosaur discoverers – G.A.

First published 2022 by Nosy Crow Ltd
The Crow's Nest, 14 Baden Place, Crosby Row, London, SE1 1YW, UK

Nosy Crow Eireann Ltd
44 Orchard Grove, Kenmare, Co Kerry, V93 FY22, Ireland

www.nosycrow.com

ISBN 978 1 83994 494 9 (HB)
ISBN 978 1 83994 495 6 (PB)

A CIP catalogue record for this book is available from the British Library.

Printed in Italy
Papers used by Nosy Crow are made from wood grown in sustainable forests.

1 3 5 7 9 8 6 4 2 (HB)
1 3 5 7 9 8 6 4 2 (PB)

THIS IS NOT A DINOSAUR!

BARRY TIMMS

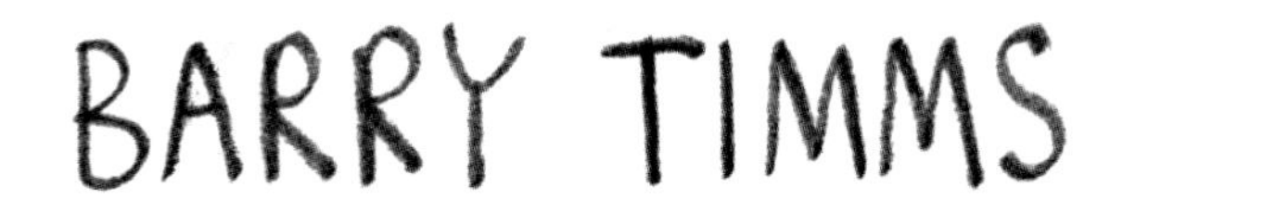

GED ADAMSON

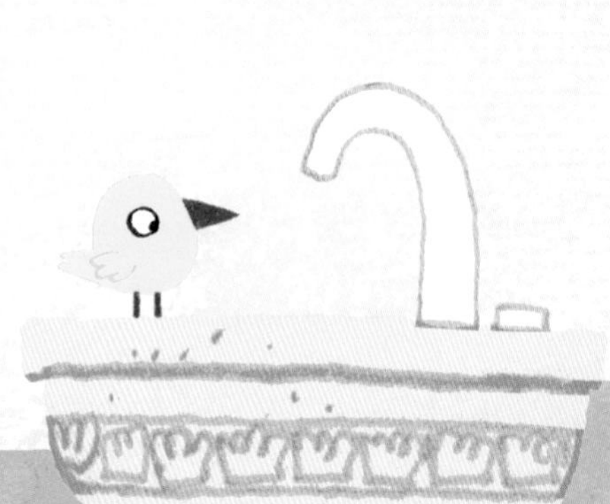

Hey there, you!
Look over here –
you won't believe your eyes.
A very special creature
wants to play with you . . .

. . . SURPRISE!

It isn't like the other beasts
you may have seen before.
It might seem prehistoric . . .

but it's **NOT** a dinosaur.

It's a . . .

. . . sign-osaur.

A shine-osaur.

A very-grand-design-osaur.

A clever-magic-trick-osaur.

A supersonic-kick-osaur!

Well, goodness me!
Whatever next?
Let's play a little more.
Expect the unexpected –

this is **NOT** a dinosaur!

It's a . . .

. . . leap-osaur.

A sleep-osaur.
Z
z
z
z
Z
Z
Z
z

A dive-into-the-deep-osaur.

A helpful-with-your-hair-osaur.

An ENTER-IF-YOU-DARE-osaur!

This animal's amazing!
It's got fun and games galore.
But one thing is for certain –

this is **NOT** a dinosaur!

It's a . . .

. . . glide-osaur.

A hide-osaur.

A sail-the-ocean-wide-osaur.
A brave-and-noble-
knight-osaur.

A hold-on-really-tight-osaur!

A wipe-your-tears-
away-osaur.

A make-a-better-
day-osaur.

A rocky-mountain-climb-osaur.

A travel-back-
in-time-osaur!

This creature is ASTONISHING.
Unique! One of a kind.

But who will take good care
of such a rare and precious find?

Think-osaur . . .

think-osaur . . .

What’s-the-missing-link-osaur?

Have-you-worked-it-out-osaur?
Quickly-shout-it-out-osaur!

This animal wants YOU
to be its very special friend.

So don't delay – just proudly say . . .

. . . "You're mine-osaur!"

The end.